For Paul,
Malia, and
Nicholas
love, G.G.

Copyright © 1995 by Martha Alexander
All rights reserved.
First edition 1995

Library of Congress Cataloging-in-Publication Data
Alexander, Martha G.
You're a genius, Blackboard Bear / Martha Alexander.—1st U.S. ed.
Summary: Blackboard Bear helps a small boy build a spaceship for a trip to the moon, but
when the boy packs so many supplies that there is no room for him, the bear goes alone.
ISBN 1-56402-238-2
[1. Space flight to the moon—Fiction. 2. Bears—Fiction.] I. Title
PZ7.A3777Yo   1995
[E]—dc20   94-11060

10 9 8 7 6 5 4 3 2 1

Printed in Italy

The pictures in this book were done in pencil and watercolor.

Candlewick Press
2067 Massachusetts Avenue
Cambridge, Massachusetts 02140

You're a Genius,
BLACKBOARD
BEAR

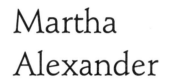

Martha
Alexander

CANDLEWICK PRESS
CAMBRIDGE, MASSACHUSETTS

The moon sounds great! Can we go there, Dad?

But, Anthony, I don't know how to build a spaceship.

What are you doing, Blackboard Bear? It's the middle of the night.

A spaceship? Really? You're drawing the parts? Wow!

Oh, I see. You're going to put it together outside. Can I help?

WE DID IT! You're a genius!

Do we need to go right away? What if we get lost?

Oh, you drew a compass to show us how to get there.

It looks like the moon is all covered with snow.
I'd better get my snow suit and mittens and sleeping bag.

I hope the moon isn't too bumpy. I'll miss my warm bed.

I bet there's no water up there.

And there's probably nothing to eat either.

Do you think there are any monsters on the moon?
You don't really know?

Oh, . . . uh . . . well . . . uh, it looks like there's no room for me.
I guess I won't be able to go.

You'll go alone and see what it's like on the moon?
You wouldn't be afraid without me?

Be careful now. Don't bump into any stars.

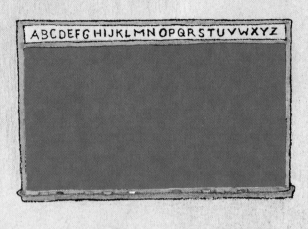